To our parents—Wilbur and CleoMae Dungy, and Doris
and Leonard Harris—for teaching us the value of friendships.
And to our children—Tiara, James, Eric,
Jordan, Jade, Justin, and Jason for continuing that legacy.

We would like to give a special thank you to Nathan Whitaker,
Dee Ann Grand, and Ron Mazellan, who helped
turn the ideas in our minds into words and pictures on paper.
It was a joy and a blessing to work with you! —L. D. and T. D.

To Kyle and Ashley, be strong and always courageous. —R. M.

*The Lord does not look at the things man looks at. Man looks
at the outward appearance, but the Lord looks at the heart.*
1 Samuel 16:7 (NIV)

LITTLE SIMON INSPIRATIONS
An imprint of Simon & Schuster Children's Publishing Division
1230 Avenue of the Americas, New York, New York 10020
Text copyright © 2011 by Tony and Lauren Dungy • Illustrations copyright © 2011 by Ron Mazellan
Published in association with the literary agency of Legacy, LLC, Winter Park, FL 32789
LITTLE SIMON INSPIRATIONS and associated colophon are trademarks of Simon & Schuster, Inc.
For information about special discounts for bulk purchases, please contact
Simon & Schuster Special Sales at 1-866-506-1949 or business@simonandschuster.com.
The Simon & Schuster Speakers Bureau can bring authors to your live event.
For more information or to book an event contact the Simon & Schuster Speakers Bureau
at 1-866-248-3049 or visit our website at www.simonspeakers.com.
Designed by Leyah Jensen • Manufactured in the United States of America 1210 PCR
Cataloging-in-Publication Data for this title is available from the Library of Congress.
First Edition • 2 4 6 8 10 9 7 5 3 1 • ISBN 978-1-4169-9771-9

# TONY & LAUREN DUNGY

# You Can Be a Friend

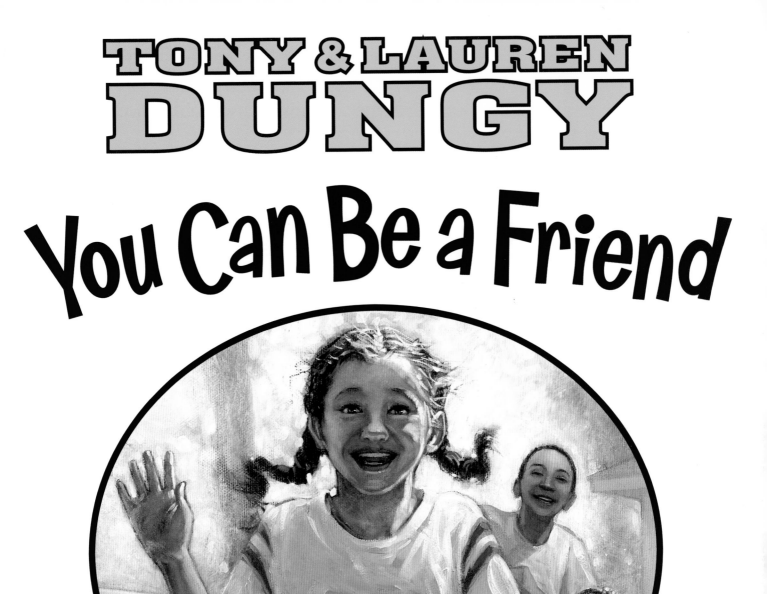

## Illustrated by Ron Mazellan

LITTLE SIMON INSPIRATIONS
New York    London    Toronto    Sydney

It was a hot day. A hot and sticky day. The kind of day when you've got to eat your ice-cream cone fast before it melts down onto your fingers.

Jordan stood still, not able to move.
In fact he was frozen in place. He had been
tagged by Jade in their game of freeze.

Justin ran and hid behind a tree across the street, trying to figure out how he could get past his speedy sister, Jade, without getting tagged so he could "unfreeze" his brother.

"Car!" shouted Jade.

All of the children took a time-out as a car slowly drove toward them, finally turning into the driveway across the street. It was followed by a huge moving truck that blocked the whole cul-de-sac because it was too big to turn into the driveway.

They raced into the house, forgetting that they were in the middle of a freeze tag game, shouting with excitement.

"Mom! Mom! Somebody's moving in!"

Mom paused and turned to face them. "Do you know who?"

They shook their heads. Jade said, "None of us got a look at them before their car went behind the bushes."

"I did," said Jordan, "and I saw a girl's face in the back window!"

"Really?" Jade asked eagerly. "What did she look like? Was she my age?"

"I couldn't really tell, Jade," Jordan said. "All I could see was brown hair."

Jade was thrilled!
She was usually the only
girl around and wished
there was at least one
other girl nearby that she
could have on her team.

"Well," said Mom,
"girls or boys,
we're happy to have
new neighbors.
All that unpacking
must be making
them hungry, so let's
bake cookies."

Mom gathered everyone in the kitchen, and put the kids to work. Jade measured, Justin poured, and Jordan mixed the ingredients.

Jade kept daydreaming about the new girl across the street.

"Mom!" she said. "Do you think the new girl will be in my class?"

"Maybe," said Mom.

"Do you think the new girl will come to my birthday party?"

"I'm sure she'd appreciate an invitation," said Mom, smiling.
"I'd appreciate cookies," said Jordan.

"Can we try one?" asked Justin. "Because unpacking makes you hungry. But making cookies makes *me* hungry."
Everyone laughed as Mom passed the cookies around, and they all took a bite.

Yuck! They were terrible!

"Uh-oh," Jade said, and she pointed at the ingredients still on the counter. Instead of sugar she had used salt! "I was so busy thinking about my new friend, I guess I wasn't paying attention."

As soon as the new batch of cookies was ready, they sampled a few to make sure they were sweet and yummy.

"Delicious," Mom said, and then they all headed across the street and rang the doorbell.

"Hi. We're the Dungys, your neighbors across the street," said Mom. "We wanted to say how happy we are that you are here."

"We even brought cookies!" Justin said. Jade and Jordan were trying to look past the doorway. All they could see were stacks of moving boxes blocking the hallway.

"Oh, thank you! We're the Snells," said their new neighbor. "Girls, you have friends here to meet!" she called.

A girl came out onto the porch. "Hi, I'm Elise!" the girl said. *She's not the girl that I saw through the car window, Jordan thought.*

Jade and Justin looked into the house. A second girl came into view—wheeling her wheelchair around the boxes. "Sorry, Mom. I was trying to find my bowling ball when you called me."

She then turned toward the family. "Hi, I'm Hannah!"

"Welcome to the neighborhood, Hannah," the kids said.

"Well," said Mom, "you let us know when you settle in. We're looking forward to having you as neighbors."

That evening the family drove to the library as they often did. Jade had been quiet all afternoon, but finally she spoke up. "Mom, do I have to be Hannah's friend? She can't do any of the things that my friends and I do."

Mom and Dad looked at each other, and Dad spoke softly. "That's not the best reason to be friends. You should be friends with someone because of the *kind* of person that they are. Let's find some activities to do with Hannah to get to know her better."

Mom added, "God made everyone, and we are all special in His eyes. Sometimes we might have to look a little harder to see that."

"But will she be *fun?*" Jade asked.

"Remember when Jordan broke his leg and had to be in a cast and wheelchair?" Mom replied. "He still was able to do lots of things-including going to the school dance, which turned out to be a terrific time."

Jordan piped up. "What about bowling? She was unpacking a bowling ball!"

"Now, that's a great idea," said Dad. "Why don't we ask the Snells if Hannah wants to go bowling with us?"

"Well . . . ," said Jade. "I guess we could ask."

Two days later they were at the bowling alley. Mom looked over, and saw Jade and Hannah sharing a lane, taking turns rolling the ball. Jade's ball went slowly down the lane, then down into the gutter.

"This is boring!" said Jade.

"Jade, try it this time with your third and fourth fingers in the holes. That should let you roll it harder and straighter," said Hannah.

Sure enough, Jade's next ball sped right down the middle!

"Yay!" yelled Jade. "It worked!"

Jade and Hannah spent the rest of the game laughing and practicing their aim at the pins. When they were done, Jade smiled at Hannah. "Now that was a blast!" she said.

Hannah smiled back. "Now that you can knock some down, next time I'll show you how to use the scoreboard."

"I can't wait!" said Jade.

Over the next several days Jade and Hannah spent much of their time together. Jade was pleased to find out that Hannah was fun—*really* fun to be around. They played games, shared secrets, and giggled—a lot. Jade was amazed at how much Hannah knew about animals, too.

One day Jordan snatched Jade's stuffed dinosaur and ran with it.
"I have your dinosaur!" he teased from down the hall.
"Give it back!" Jade yelled.

"Jordan," said Hannah calmly. "That is a *Tyrannosaurus rex*, and as a meat eater, he will eat all of your other animals unless you give him back." Jordan threw him back down the hall, and Jade and Hannah gave each other a big high five.

Then Hannah looked up at the calendar in Jade's room. "Hey, your birthday is coming up soon."

Jade was startled for a moment. "How did you know that?" she asked. Hannah laughed. "Well, you have a big red circle around the day on your calendar with the words MY BIRTHDAY! written underneath it," she said. "I *love* to go to parties!"

Jade smiled at Hannah but felt uneasy. "Me too," she said.

A few nights later their older brother, Eric, heard Jade and Jordan arguing. Jordan saw him and called out to him. "Eric, can you answer a question for us?"

"Sure. What's up, J?"
"Jade can't decide if she should invite Hannah to her birthday party next week."
"Isn't Hannah the new girl across the street?" They nodded.
Eric looked at Jade. "Haven't you been spending a lot of time with her lately?"
"Yes," Jade said. "But I've been planning my birthday at the water park *forever*, and if I invite Hannah . . ."

Jade paused, then said, "She'll either be by herself some of the time, or I will have to stay with her and . . ."

"You're afraid that if you invite her, then you won't be able to go on the big slides, to surfboard, or go off the diving boards." Eric knew Jade loved to do all of those things but wouldn't want to leave anybody out. "You're really asking if it is more important to have fun at your party or to be with your friends," Eric said. "I can't answer that, Jade. Only you can."

"I know. I've been thinking about it all week," Jade said.

Eric paused and stared at his brother and sister, saying, "One more thing . . ." They looked up at him, a bit worried. "You're being way too serious!" Eric jumped on the bed and began tickling and wrestling his brother and sister.

The next morning Jade walked into the kitchen for breakfast and announced, "Mom, I don't want to have my party at the water park."

"But that's all you've talked about for months, Jade. You have really been excited about going there for your birthday."

"I know. But now I want to have my party at the zoo."

"Are you sure?" Mom asked.

"Yes. That way Hannah can go to the party, too, and won't feel left out the way she might if we went to the water park. I can always go to the water park another time. Eric said that I had to decide if I wanted to have fun on my birthday or be with my friends. And by moving my party to the zoo, I can do both!"

"I think that's a great idea," said Mom, and she gave Jade a hug.

"You know what, Mom?" said Jade. "I think this is going to be my best birthday yet."

And it was.
Hannah and Jade
both thought so.

One of the best lessons our parents taught us as children was to be friendly to everyone. That's something we've tried to pass on to our kids.

Sometimes we see people and we don't think they'll be friendly or fun because of the way they look. We don't try to make friends with them because they're different. Jade almost made that mistake with Hannah because of her wheelchair.

Jade's parents helped her get to know Hannah because that's what God wants us to do. He loves everyone, and He wants us to love everyone, too.

You can be a friend, too!

*Lauren Dungy*

*Tony Dungy*